CONTENTS

1. SAD LIFE
2. NEW FAMILY
3. MY NAMES
4. NAUGHTY HUNNI
5. GET THE HOSE OUT
6. HAPPY HUNNI
7. MAGPIE
8. HUNNI ON HOLIDAY
9. ADVENTURES IN THE HIGHLANDS
10. SORE PAW
11. LOST IN WOODS
12. HAPPY LIFE

1. SAD LIFE

I can still remember my life before my new Mummy and Daddy that I live with now. I was left on my own all day when they went out.

I got bored and hungry so I would look around the house for something to eat.

I can open doors if I jump up and hit the handle with my paw. I can open the bin if I flip the lid with my nose.

Sometimes, the bin would tip over though and make a mess. I was so hungry one day I chewed a pair of my sisters shoes, she didn't give me a row but my Daddy smacked me hard and I didn't get any dinner. I was so scared of him. He was always shouting at Mummy and she would cry.

I would keep my wee and poo in all day then I would have an accident. I would get into big trouble for that too.

When Mummy, Daddy and Susan came home I would be so pleased to see them, jumping up and wagging my tail. Daddy would shout at me but Mummy and Susan would be nice to me and tell Daddy to stop.

Most of my walks were at the weekend or I got put out in the garden.

Susan would play with me. At night-time I would sleep under the table on the cold floor.

I didn't like my life and was a very sad dog.

2. NEW FAMILY

Just after Christmas a big man came to my house to take me away. I was scared but he seemed kind, he was my new Daddy. He took me to see my new Mummy who was at work; she was so pleased to see me. I jumped on her and licked her. She seemed to like me a lot.

When I arrived at my new house there was another dog there called Tilly. She was staying with us as her Daddy was away on holiday. She was like me but all black and a bit older than me. I sniffed around looking for food. My new Daddy took us for a big walk at the airport fields and I met other dogs like me so that was fun.

Daddy kept me on the lead, I think he was scared I would run away, I wouldn't have as I didn't know where I was.

When we got back Daddy put a noisy machine on to have a drink of coffee, I didn't like the noise so I barked very loudly to tell him to stop then hid under the table.

He said "It's okay Hunni, don't worry."

I growled and showed him my teeth. He said "No Hunni, that's bad."

Mummy came home from work and made a big fuss of me, I was so pleased to see her. Then I met the rest of my new family, Liam and Rebekah, my big sister and brother who cuddled and played with me for ages. They brought me some toys and told me to be nice to them when I wanted to chew them. I liked the squeaky ones the best.

3. MY NAMES

I have lots of names but my proper name is Hunni. Sometimes, I get called Chicken, Pigeon, Bubba, Snoopy, Poopy, Puppy, Come here and Sit.

I am allowed off the lead now and I like to play with the ball or frisbee. I get it thrown for me and I chase it. If I bring it back I get a biscuit, it's a good game. I never want it to end but I get tired.

Before, when I was out in the rain and I got wet and I didn't like getting dried, Daddy would bend over me and I got scared so I growled at him. He said "Bad dog, in your bed."

Mummy said "You shouldn't get angry with her, she's scared, just walk away and ignore her."

When Mummy dried me she bent down beside me and I gave her one paw at a time. I didn't growl at her. Daddy is better at drying me now.

A few times when everyone was out I could smell something nice in the bin so I flipped the lid up with my nose but it fell over. When mummy and Daddy came home I knew I had been bad so I hid under the table shaking and growling.

They said "Aw Hunni, what did u do? It's okay." Daddy tried to pat me but I growled and showed my teeth. Daddy just walked away.

I heard Mummy and Daddy talking one day, Daddy said, " I don't think we can keep her, I'm not putting up with this, lets phone the Dog's Trust and get her re-homed.

I was so upset and I thought I need to be good, but sometimes I get so scared. Scared of smacks, scared of loud noises and scared of not getting fed.

I heard Daddy on the phone to Dog's Trust saying that I didn't like him and that I growled and snapped at him, I didn't mean it.

He came off the phone and said to Mummy "Probably 4-6 weeks" Mummy was crying but said she understood.

4. NAUGHTY HUNNI

Four weeks was up and I had been good I think. I heard them talking and they said they would give me another chance, I was so happy and thought I would try to be a good dog.

Mummy and daddy got a cage for me, I wasn't happy  at first but then I quite liked my wee space, I felt safe.

After a year I was given a fluffy bed and the bin was put in the garage. Mummy and Daddy always checked the kitchen to make sure there was nothing I could eat. Although one day they left a very tasty lasagne on the top of the cooker with a cover on it; I smelt it all day and was very hungry, I couldn't help myself, I jumped up and ate it and it was yummy. I then thought, "Oops I'm in big trouble."

Mummy came in and said" Aw Hunni, what have you done, that was our dinner."

I hid under the table; she said "It's okay Hunni."

I heard her on the phone to Daddy laughing that I had eaten their tea. Humans are always eating, it's not fair, I'm always hungry and they call ME greedy.

Another time my Auntie Gill was looking after me, she left me in the kitchen when she went out for a little while. When she was out I could smell the chocolate brownies she had made. I was drooling they smelt so good. I jumped up and knocked the box onto the floor, I chewed the lid to open it then I ate them all.

Auntie Gill came back and said "Oh no Hunni, what have you done? That's bad." I ran and hid under the table, she just ignored me but I didn't get any dinner. For once I wasn't hungry anyway.

Her daughter Tegan and son Brandon played with me all the time, it was great fun.

5. GET THE HOSE OUT

Mummy and Daddy let me off the lead once they could trust me but one day Daddy opened the back gate and let me out.

Mummy said "Don't do that, she might run away but Daddy said," she will be fine"

He was wrong; I decided to run towards the woods, not too far, I could smell something good so I rolled in it. I could hear Mummy, Daddy and Rebekah shouting on me. I knew they weren't far away so I just ignored them as I was having far too much fun. Then a man shouted "She's over here"

Mummy found me and put a lead on me. She said "Thank you to the man then "Oh Hunni what have you rolled in? You stink"

The man said "I think its fox poo."

When I got back daddy hosed me down, I didn't like that at all. After that I wasn't allowed out the gate on my own.

Another time I jumped over into next door's garden. Mummy and Daddy said, "Hunni come back here. I barked at them to say "Chase me, chase me, I want to play" but they seemed annoyed at me. Then Mummy said "Hunni, Dentistick" so I jumped back over. She didn't give me one, I think it was a trick but I couldn't have been sure.

I usually get a row for barking too much but don't they realise that I'm trying to tell them something.

6. HAPPY HUNNI

Everyone thinks I'm cute when they talk to me; I turn my head to the side and give them a paw. I can do both paws; I'm very clever you know.

My last owners didn't teach me much, only to jump up and give a paw. Now I get a row for jumping up.

I never used to like cuddles but I do now. I sometimes sit on Daddy's knee and he strokes me. I'm not scared of Daddy anymore.

I get very excited when we get visitors; I jump on them and wag my tail. Sometimes I bark loudly and get a row-huh! I'm not allowed to talk; Mummy and Rebekah never stop talking-poor Daddy and Liam.

My boyfriend is called Tyson, he is a very handsome boy and he's tall, white and brown. We like chasing each other, sometimes he runs away; he is younger than me and not as well behaved yet.

I'm always tired after Tyson and I have had a good run, as my Mummy and Mary chat quite a lot.

My other friend is Dude who is a dog down the road, he does this funny howling thing but I like him a lot. Sometimes we take him with us on our walk.

My big sister Rebekah took me to Cramond on a bus. It was my first time on a bus and nobody seemed to mind when I climbed onto the seat and sat down, they all laughed. We went to the beach and I chased the ball and ran in the sea I loved it. Rebekah shared her cheese and pickle sandwich with me. I liked the cheese and bread, but not the pickle. Then we shared the ice cream, well Rebekah tried to share it with me but I ate most of it, yum, yum!

7. MAGPIE

One day I was in the garden when I saw a bird in the corner, it looked like my toy Grousey so I pounced on it as I wanted to play. I had it in my mouth when Mummy screamed, "NO Hunni."

I dropped it, ran inside and hid under the table.

Mummy was crying and she said" Oh Hunni, what have you done, the poor bird." She lifted the bird up and put it in a box, it was in shock. I was put in another room.

An hour later a lady in uniform came to the door from the SSPCA to pick up the bird. I heard her saying, "Your dog didn't do anything wrong, I think the bird was already injured and that's why it didn't fly away."

That was good news as I didn't mean to hurt it, I just wanted to play. I wondered if the bird would come back to our garden or it was too scared. I like chasing things, if a pussycat came into my garden, I would chase it away its MY GARDEN!

One day my Mummy and Daddy had friends round for dinner. They left the garage door open; I could smell a pussycat along the street so I ran to find it and chased it in its garden. Then  I heard Mummy, Daddy, Liam, Rebekah and their friends shouting "Hunni, Hunni." I just ignored them because I was having so much fun. Then the man came out of the house and said "She's in our garden" I thought I would have got a row but everyone was pleased to see me. Mummy gave Daddy a row for leaving the garage door open.

8. HUNNI ON HOLIDAY

My humans sometimes leave me with my Auntie Laura and Uncle Trevor when they go on holiday. I like it there as we go up the hills and to the beach. Uncle Trevor plays with me a lot, we play tuggy where I have a toy in my mouth and he tries to pull it off me, its great fun.

The last time I stayed with them we went to Holyrood Park and I rolled in fox poo, it smelt so good. Auntie Laura tied me to the fence in the street and ran up and down stairs with basins of water, she didn't have any dog shampoo so she washed me with human shampoo. Yuk it was stinky but Mummy and Daddy liked it they said it was "Molton Brown", whatever that means.

We also went to the pub. Auntie Laura and Uncle Trevor had food and beer and I sat under the table hoping for crumbs, I got a few chips, yummy! A few other dogs came in, they were all very friendly.

After three days my Mummy and Daddy came back  to get me. I had a nice time but I was so excited to see them and go home. I was very tired with all the big walks and playing but I got to go in the car! Also I don't sleep well when I'm away because I hear noises that I'm not used to.

9. ADVENTURES IN THE HIGHLANDS

My humans took me to visit Auntie Mo and Uncle Dave in Fort William. I had been there before when I  was younger. They had two collie dog's called Polo and Belle but Polo died. I liked them a lot and was sad about Polo. Then they got a new dog called Skye who didn't like me very much.

We had a big fight over a Frisbee so Auntie Mo pulled us apart by our tails and put us in separate car boots until we calmed down, all the humans were upset with us.

I kept trying to be Skye's friend but she just didn't

like me. The next time we went to visit, Skye had a muzzle on her mouth and nose so I felt safer. By the end of the stay we were becoming friends, she was learning that I was a nice dog. We went lovely big walks down by the river and up the hills.

The last time we met Skye was pleased to see me and sadly Belle had died so they had a new dog called Nan who was a bit unsure of me. I just kept wagging my tail at her to show her I was friendly.

We went over to Knoydart and I had lots of fun with Skye, Nan and a wee puppy called Turbo.

I like going holidays as long as my Mummy and Daddy are with me but I am always glad to get home.

10. SORE PAW

When my Mummy and daddy went to Spain I stayed with Auntie Laura and Uncle Trevor again, I like going there.

On the third day I was out with Uncle Trevor on the lead and I went into long grass to do the toilet, I stood on something sharp and my back paw got stuck. It was very sore and I pulled Uncle Trevor back to his house. When we got back they tried to have a look but I was growling to tell them that it was too sore and please don't touch it.

One of the neighbours came upstairs with some bandages and Trevor fed me biscuits while Laura bandaged my paw. The next day they took me to the vet, I don't remember much but I think they put me to sleep so as they could clean my paw and put a bandage on. I got something for the pain too.

I just wanted my Mummy and Daddy and I was really sad, I couldn't go walks, only out for the toilet, not much fun. I had to go back to the vet three times to get a new bandage; I didn't like it and was scared.

On the Saturday, Laura and Trevor took me home and waited in the house for Mummy and Daddy. I was so pleased to see them and glad to be home.

The first week Daddy was with me all the time, took me to the vet and gave me lots of cuddles then Daddy went away to London. I was sad again but then Rebekah came home, I got more cuddles and tummy rubs.

One morning when Mummy and Rebekah were sleeping my paw was very itchy so I chewed the bandage off and ate the honey dressing, it was very tasty. Mummy and Rebekah came downstairs and said, "Oh no Hunni what have you done?" I hid under the table shaking. My mummy bandaged it again then she put a towel round my neck and taped it on, I didn't like it, it was to stop me from doing it again. A few days later I was left on my own most of the day 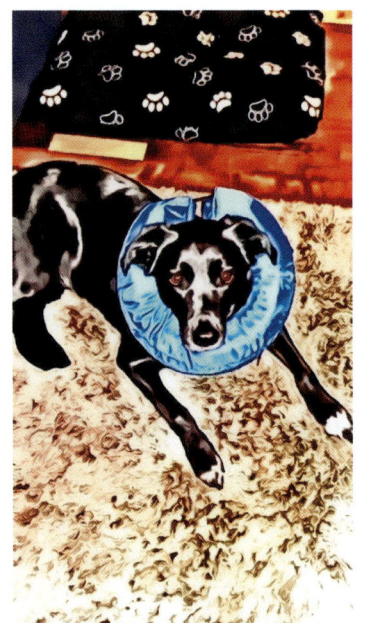 because mummy and Rebekah were working, I was bored and my paw was sore and itchy, I managed to chew my bandage off again and eat the honey, yum yum. Mummy came in from work and said, "Oh no

Hunni, what have you done, not again." Then Mummy bandaged it again and went to Pets at Home to get me a buster collar so as I couldn't reach my paw, it looked like a swimming rubber ring that goes around my neck, I didn't like it. It only went on when I was on my own.

One night I was finding it hard to sleep so I had to rearrange my whole bed until I was comfy, it took quite a while, Mummy and Rebekah said I was very clever.

Two more visits to the vet then my paw was healed and I could get back to my walks thank goodness.

11. LOST IN THE WOODS

My Auntie Brush and Uncle Byron came to stay before they went to Oz (whatever that means, I'm not sure but it's far away.) My Auntie Brush took me a walk when my Mummy and Daddy were at work. Her nickname is Brush because she flicked her hair in a big sweeping wave with a hair brush when she was younger.

We walked around the Norton then I pulled her up the woods. It was great fun, she threw the ball for me and I sniffed in the bushes.

After a while Auntie Brush looked worried and said. "Hunni I'm lost, take me home. I thought that was funny because she was supposed to be looking after me, but it was okay because I know my way home so it was easy. She put me on the lead and I showed her the way home. I was in charge for once and I quite liked it.

I liked my Auntie and Uncle staying because there was always someone in the house and I got extra walks and cuddles. I was sad when they went away to Oz. I sometimes sit on my bench waiting for them to come back.

12. HAPPY LIFE

I love my life now and I love my Daddy so much, I get upset when he leaves me. He gives me lots of pats, cuddles and the best walks. I also love seeing Liam  and Rebekah when they come home, I run about all excited. Mummy usually works out what I need and she feeds me when I stare at her for a while, usually an hour before dinner. Sometimes she gives in and feeds me earlier. Mummy says "everything's fine and dandy" but who is Dandy? My life is walking, playing, eating, cuddles and sleeping. It's a dog's life and I wouldn't change it for anything, well maybe some more food!

Printed in Poland
by Amazon Fulfillment
Poland Sp. z o.o., Wrocław